the

Sea Turtle

A Random House book
Published by Random House Australia Pty Ltd
Level 3, 100 Pacific Highway, North Sydney NSW 2060

www.randomhouse.com.au

First published by Random House Australia in 2014
Copyright © Belinda Murrell 2014
Illustrations copyright © Serena Geddes 2014

Addresses for companies within the Random House Group can be found at www.randomhouse.com.au/offices

National Library of Australia
Cataloguing-in-Publication Entry

Author: Murrell, Belinda
Title: Lulu Bell and the sea turtle/Belinda Murrell; illustrated by Serena Geddes
ISBN: 978 0 85798 201 8 (paperback)
Series: Murrell, Belinda. Lulu Bell; 6
Target audience: For primary school age
Subjects: Sea turtles – Juvenile fiction
Other authors/contributors: Geddes, Serena
Dewey number: A823.4

Cover and internal illustrations by Serena Geddes
Cover design by Christabella Designs
Internal design and typesetting in 16/22 pt Bembo by Ingo Voss, based on series design by Anna Warren, Warren Ventures
Printed in Australia by Griffin Press, an accredited ISO AS/NZS 14001:2004 Environmental Management System printer

Random House Australia uses papers that are natural, renewable and recyclable products and made from wood grown in sustainable forests. The logging and manufacturing processes are expected to conform to the environmental regulations of the country of origin.

Lulu Bell and the Sea Turtle

Belinda Murrell

Illustrated by Serena Geddes

RANDOM HOUSE AUSTRALIA

Lulu   Dad

Mum   Gus   Rosie

For Maureen, Frank and Ashley, and all
the Gambanan kids – Keelan, Manton, Pot,
Marika, Karen, Maureen, Liam, Isiah, Selwyn,
and Hakim. Thank you!

Chapter 1

Exciting News

It was dinnertime and the Bell family was seated around the kitchen table. Mum had made lemon roast chicken, roast vegetables and crunchy green salad. It was one of Lulu's favourite meals.

'Mmmm,' said Lulu. 'This is delicious. Thanks, Mum.'

'*Dulishus,*' agreed her little brother Gus. He popped a whole roast potato into his mouth. His cheeks bulged as he chewed.

'Thanks, honey buns,' said Mum.
'I'm glad you're enjoying it. I thought we should celebrate. I had some *very* exciting news today.'

Dad grinned. 'We love exciting news. Don't we, kids?'

'I have been asked to organise a very special art show for the local gallery,' said Mum.

Lulu's mum Chrissie was an artist. She created the most wonderful paintings. Her work was sold at several galleries.

'That's great,' said Dad. 'What's the art show about?'

Mum smiled. Her cheeks were pink with delight. 'It is a collection by Aboriginal artists from the far north of Western Australia,' she explained. 'It will be the first time their work has been shown here.'

Mum glanced around the table at the family. 'I've been asked to fly over there to meet the artists. I have to interview them about their work and decide on a theme. Then I'll choose the artworks and organise for them to be shipped over.'

Lulu felt a little flutter of nerves. Mum was going away. *Who would look after them while Dad was at work? Who would look after Gus while they were at school?*

'That *is* exciting,' said Dad. 'When do you have to go?'

Mum gave a big grin. 'I've asked the gallery owner if I can go next week. It's the school holidays then. That means you can all come with me. It will be an amazing adventure.'

'We're going to Western Australia for the holidays?' cried Lulu. That *did* sound like an adventure.

'Will we go on a plane?' asked Lulu's younger sister Rosie.

'Asha and Jessie come too?' added Gus. The two dogs pricked up their ears at the sound of their names. Jessie gave a big doggy smile. She was always keen for an adventure.

Mum laughed. 'No, the dogs can't come with us, honey bun.' She turned to Rosie. 'Yes, we will go on a plane. We'll fly to Broome. It's on the north coast of Western Australia. Then we'll drive about two hundred kilometres further north to a tiny Aboriginal community called Ardyaloon.'

Dad rubbed his chin. 'It's a long way to go,' he said. 'And we'd have to find someone to look after the vet hospital.'

Dad was a vet. The family lived right behind Shelly Beach Veterinary Hospital.

'Please, Dad?' begged Lulu. 'Can we go? Kylie could feed all the animals.'

Dad thought about it. 'She certainly could. And I could ask Dr Humphrey to see the patients for me.' Kylie was the vet nurse, and Dr Humphrey was a retired vet who sometimes helped out.

Dad grinned. 'Let's do it!'

'Hurray,' cried Lulu, Rosie and Gus together.

'Where will we stay?' asked Lulu.

'I spoke to Harry today. He's one of the Aboriginal elders,' said Mum. 'He invited us to camp on his family's property. Their land is on the beach just west of Ardyaloon.'

Lulu jiggled with excitement.

'I'll have to work for a few days. But we'll also make it a lovely family holiday. We can go swimming and boating and explore the islands,' said Mum.

'And fishing and watching wildlife,' added Dad. 'We might even get to see saltwater crocodiles or sea turtles.'

'It *will* be an amazing adventure!' agreed Lulu. 'I can't wait.'

Chapter 2

The Journey

Lulu thought the holidays would never come. The last week of school seemed to take forever.

Finally it was Saturday morning. Dad woke them all early. Gus yawned and pulled his Bug Boy mask down over his face.

Lulu was excited but a little sad too. It was hard to say goodbye to all the pets. She cuddled Flopsy the rabbit in the garden. She fed the four ducklings.

Then she went inside and crawled under her bed. The family cats, Pickles and Pepper, were hiding there.

The dogs were most unhappy. Asha was sulking on her bed. Lulu hugged her. Asha wiggled her tail the tiniest bit.

'It's okay, girl,' said Lulu. 'We'll be back soon.'

Jessie sat by the door and drooped. She was usually the smiliest dog in the world. But not today.

'Don't worry, sweetheart,' said Dad
to Lulu. 'Kylie will take good care of
them all.'

Nanna and Gumpa came to drive
them to the airport. Gumpa helped Dad
pack the bags in the car. Lulu could only
take what she could fit in her backpack.

Then they were off. Nanna and Gumpa dropped them out the front of the airport. Everyone kissed and waved. Nanna gave Lulu a super-big hug.

'Have fun, my darling Lulu,' whispered Nanna. 'I'll miss you.'

'I'll miss you too, Nanna.' Lulu could feel a lump in her throat.

'Goodbye. Love you. See you soon,' Mum called to her parents.

Mum held Gus tightly by the hand in the airport. Soon they were on the plane. Lulu clicked on her seatbelt. Rosie wriggled beside her.

The flight took hours. The cabin crew brought around breakfast on trays. There were lots of little packages to open. Lulu ate fruit salad and yoghurt and a warm omelette. Dad, Lulu and Rosie watched movies on a small screen

on the back of the seat. Gus slept. Then
they ate lunch. At last the plane began to
descend. Lulu could see a vast blue ocean
shining below.

As they walked off the plane in
Broome, the heat hit Lulu like a wave.
It was humid and sticky.

Their first stop was to pick up the car. Mum had organised to rent a big four-wheel drive. It towed a low camper trailer. This was to be their home for the next week.

Their second stop was the shopping centre. Everyone helped do the grocery shopping. Then it all had to be packed away in the trailer. Finally the family and their gear were loaded in the car.

'Only another three hours to go,' said Mum. 'Ardyaloon, here we come.'

The road north was rough, rutted red dirt. On either side grew thick green scrub. Overhead arched a sky of deepest blue. Lulu had never felt so far from home.

It was a long, bumpy drive. Rosie and Gus fell asleep. Lulu read her book. It was early evening when they finally arrived.

Mum turned the car onto a sidetrack.
A sign beside the gate read 'Goorlil'.

'Here it is,' cried Mum. 'Goorlil.
It means "turtle" in the local Bardi
language.'

Lulu shivered with excitement.

What adventures would they find at Goorlil?

Chapter 3

The Goorlil Family

The car rounded a bend in the track.

The first thing Lulu saw was the sea. Deep turquoise-blue stretched all the way to the horizon. Dozens of red rock islands jutted from the water. Rich green mangroves hugged the coast. A pod of dolphins swam by, diving and splashing.

'Oooh,' cried Lulu. 'Look at that!'

The next thing Lulu saw was the house. It was a small building with a verandah across the front. To the side was a camp fire. A crowd of people were gathered around. Adults chatted. Kids laughed and played chasings. An older woman was cooking over the fire.

Mum stopped the car under a tree. 'At last,' she said.

Lulu stretched as she climbed out of the car. It had been a long journey.

A throng of people gathered around. 'Hello,' called a few voices.

'Hi, I'm Chrissie,' said Mum.

'And I'm Harry,' said an older man. He had a kind face and greying hair. 'Welcome to Goorlil.'

Mum introduced everyone in the Bell family. Harry introduced everyone in the Goorlil family. There were lots of aunts and uncles, mums and dads, grandparents and grandchildren.

For a moment Lulu felt shy. It was noisy with so many people talking at once. But everyone was so friendly that Lulu soon joined in.

'Would you like a cup of tea?' asked Harry's wife Pearl. She picked up a billy can that was bubbling over the fire. 'You must be tired.'

'That would be lovely,' agreed Mum. 'I'm exhausted.'

Mum and Dad settled into two of the camp chairs beside the fire. They began chatting with the adults about the local artists and the art show.

Lulu looked around her. Everything was so different and interesting.

'I'm Tam,' said one of the girls. She was taller than Lulu and had a lovely smile. 'This is my sister Zalie.' She pointed to a girl about the same age as Rosie. 'And these are my cousins Jacob, Zac, Eli and Joe.' She waved towards a group of boys.

The children grinned at each other. Gus looked up at the boys. They were all wearing shorts and had bare feet. He looked down at his Bug Boy costume.

'And this is our new puppy. He's called Chilli,' said Tam. The puppy wriggled and licked Lulu's fingers. Then he began to chase his tail round and round. He fell over. Lulu laughed.

The kids began to play with the puppy. Lulu noticed that Mum and Dad were now on the verandah talking to one of the men.

His name was Anthony and he was an artist. He was very tall and wore a bright red shirt.

Lulu wandered over. Mum was sipping tea from a mug. On the table beside her was a huge canvas.

'This is one of Anthony's new paintings,' explained Mum.

'It will be called *Goorlil Dreaming*,' said Anthony. 'But I've only done the background so far. This is the sea and here are the sands of the shore.'

The swirling turquoise-blue paint was the exact colour of the sea. At the bottom was a band of pale yellows.

'I'm painting the story of the turtles,' explained Anthony. 'At this time of year, the whales come to visit from down south. This means that it is also the courtship season for the turtles. The male turtles woo the females. Soon after, that the females come ashore to lay their eggs.'

Anthony traced the yellow curves of the painted beach.

'At night the turtles crawl many metres up into the warm sand dunes. They dig their nest with their flippers and lay more than a hundred eggs each. The mothers bury their eggs and crawl back to the sea. A couple of months later the eggs hatch. The babies dig their way out and head to the sea.'

'It sounds wonderful,' said Mum. 'I can't wait to see the finished painting.'

'Do you think we might see some sea turtles?' asked Lulu. 'Imagine if we saw them laying their eggs!'

Anthony smiled at Lulu. 'We might be lucky. But now I'll show you where

you are going to camp. We should set you
up before it gets dark.'

Anthony showed them a clearing in
the bush a few hundred metres past the
house. It was on a point and surrounded
by sea on two sides. The tide was low.

Down below the point was a jagged rectangular pool. It was surrounded by rough rock walls.

'Can we swim in the pool?' asked Lulu.

'That's not a pool,' said Anthony. 'It's a fish trap. It was made by our ancestors many, many years ago. As the tide drains away, fish are trapped behind. We can go down tomorrow to see if we have caught any dinner.'

He pointed to the west. 'If you want to swim in the morning, there is a little sandy beach over there.'

Anthony showed them where to fetch water and where to light the fire.

'Okay, I'll leave you to it,' he said. 'Come visit us at the house tomorrow. I'm teaching the boys how to make spears. Harry will take your mum into town to meet some of the other artists.'

'You make spears?' asked Lulu. Her brown eyes sparkled with interest.

'I teach all the boys how to hunt and fish,' explained Anthony. 'Pearl teaches the girls how to find oysters and bush tucker. And they all go to school in Ardyaloon. But they also have to learn the old ways.' He smiled at Lulu. 'You can come along to *my* school.'

'I'd love to,' said Lulu.

Chapter 4

Camp Fun

Dad and Mum set to work. The roof of the camper trailer popped up and the sides folded out to make a big raised tent. There were two double beds – one for the parents and one for the kids. The sides of the tent were made of mosquito netting so the breeze could blow through. Beyond the netting, Lulu could see the sea and the bush and the camp fire that her parents were starting.

All of the kids were given jobs to do.
Gus helped Mum make up the beds with
sleeping bags and pillows. Lulu helped
Dad to collect more wood for the fire.
Rosie set up the camp chairs.

Then Lulu and Dad cooked sausages, tomatoes and onions over the fire. Lulu's tummy rumbled at the delicious smells.

The family sat around the fire on camp chairs. As they ate dinner, the sun set over the sea to the west. The sky and sea were streaked with golds and pale purples.

'Ah,' said Mum. 'This is heaven.'

By the time the family had finished eating, it was dark. The sky was like blackest velvet spangled with millions of sparkling stars.

'I've never seen so many stars,' said Rosie.

There was no moon yet. Suddenly a line of silver streaked across the sky. It was followed by another, then another.

'There's a shooting star,' cried Lulu. 'And another one.'

'Make a wish,' said Mum. 'A trio of shooting stars must make a very powerful wish.'

'Bug Boy wish for . . .' began Gus.

'Don't tell anyone, Gus,' warned Lulu. 'Or it won't come true. Close your eyes and wish hard.'

Lulu closed her eyes. What would she wish for? She could wish for a pony. Or she could wish for a new puppy, like Chilli. But then she knew what the right wish was. She made a wish to see a sea turtle laying her eggs.

Mum took the kids to get cleaned up before bed. In the middle of the clearing was a tap with a hose. The tap was connected to a bore deep under the earth. The water came out warm and bubbly. Mum laid down a plastic mat for them to stand on to stop their clean feet getting muddy.

It felt wonderful to wash away the dust and grime of that long journey.

Lulu looked up at the blazing stars. 'This is the best shower I've ever had,' she said.

The kids dressed in their pyjamas and thongs, and walked back to the camp. They climbed into their sleeping bags on the bed. Mum read them a story. She used lots of funny voices to make them giggle.

'Another one, please, Mum?' asked Lulu hopefully.

'Pretty please, Mum?' begged Rosie.

'Sorry, honey buns. It's time for bed,' said Mum. She stood up. 'Tomorrow we have *lots* of adventures to look forward to.'

'Come tucka in, Mumma,' said Gus. He popped his thumb in his mouth.

Mum tucked them all into their sleeping bags. She kissed each one and turned the lantern off.

'I'll never get to sleep,' said Lulu. 'There is just so much to think about. Learning to make spears, searching for turtles, watching Anthony paint . . .'

But, of course, she did sleep.

Chapter 5

Making Spears

Lulu woke up and peeked out through the netting. The sun was rising over the islands to the east. Dad had already started the camp fire and was boiling the billy. Rosie and Gus were still asleep. It was a beautiful day.

Lulu jumped out of bed and dressed. She wore shorts, a shirt and her favourite boots. Then she crept outside to join Dad. Breakfast was eggs and bacon cooked over the fire.

Soon Harry arrived to take Mum into Ardyaloon to meet the other artists. Mum grabbed her camera and her notebook. She wanted to take lots of photos of the artists and their work to include in the show.

'You'd better hurry up,' Harry told Lulu. 'Anthony is already making spears.' Lulu jumped up. She didn't want to miss out. Mum kissed them all goodbye. 'Have a fun day. I'll see you this afternoon.'

'Bye, Mum,' called Lulu. 'Good luck.'

Mum and Harry drove off in Harry's four-wheel drive.

'Why don't you and Rosie walk over and meet Anthony now?' suggested Dad. 'Gus and I can do the washing up. We'll join you in a few minutes.'

So Lulu and Rosie set off for the house. Jacob's mum was sitting on the verandah drawing. Chilli the puppy was asleep at her feet.

The boys were all gathered around the fire with Anthony. Each one had a long, straight stick.

'Hello, Lulu and Rosie,' called Anthony. 'We started without you.'

Lulu looked around for Tam and Zalie. They weren't there. 'Where are the girls?' asked Lulu.

'The girls have gone out with our grandmother,' said Zac. 'She's showing them which plants to gather for bush tucker and medicine.'

'The boys have each chosen a sapling,' said Anthony. He pointed to a pile of sticks leaning against the side of the house.

Jacob explained how they had found the sticks. Anthony had helped them find long, straight wattle saplings in the bush. They had cut the saplings, stripped the bark and shaved off any bumps. The saplings had been left to dry for a couple of days.

The boys were now rubbing the wood with sandpaper.

Lulu and Rosie watched. Anthony showed the boys how to polish the wood to make it as smooth as possible.

'Then we heat sections of the wood in the fire like this,' said Anthony. He showed them with one of the saplings. 'This makes the wood soft so we can make it nice and straight. Then it sets hard.'

Anthony bent the hot wood against the table to straighten out a kink.

It was interesting to see the boys at work – polishing, heating and straightening. Dad and Gus arrived. Gus found a stick to draw in the dirt. Lulu asked Zac and Jacob lots of questions.

'What do you use the spears for?' asked Lulu. 'Are they for games?'

Zac shook his head. 'These spears aren't toys. We hunt with them.'

'Hunt?' asked Lulu. She wasn't quite sure if she believed him. 'What do you hunt?'

'Turtles, fish, stingrays,' said Zac. He mimed striking his spear at the ground.

'Oh,' said Rosie. 'The poor turtles.'

'Most of our food comes from the sea, as it always has. And we gather fruit and berries and medicine in the bush,' explained Anthony. 'We never hunt more than we need to eat. Nothing is ever wasted.'

'I don't think I'd like to eat turtle,' said Rosie. 'Don't you buy food at the shop?'

Anthony laughed. 'Some things. There is a shop in Ardyaloon where we can buy extra things we need.'

'Like chocolate,' said Zac. He rubbed his tummy and gave a cheeky grin.

Anthony nodded. 'Tomorrow I'm taking all the boys out hunting stingrays at the reef. You can come with us if you like.'

Lulu turned to Dad. 'Can we go, Dad? Pleeeease?'

'I wouldn't miss it for the world,' agreed Dad.

Dad and Anthony helped the boys to carve a point on one end of each spear with a sharp knife. One side of the point was flattened out. A deep groove was carved down the centre.

Then they put a short steel rod in the groove. The rod was lashed to the spear using fishing line.

'And now it's finished,' said Anthony.

Zac twisted his spear proudly. Gus reached for Zac's spear. 'Me go?'

Anthony looked at all the children. His face was very serious. 'You must never use anyone else's spear, unless they offer to lend it to you.'

Gus pouted. Lulu and Rosie nodded.

Anthony smiled. 'I'm going to do some painting now. We'll see you here tomorrow.'

'Thanks, Anthony,' said Lulu.

'Well, I'm a bit smoky after watching all that hard work,' said Dad as the Bell family walked back to their camp. 'I think we might go for a swim.'

The family spent the afternoon swimming and exploring. Mum came back from Ardyaloon full of stories. She had met the other artists and seen their art. She showed Lulu the photos she had taken. There were five artists whose work she would feature in the show.

Lulu loved the bright, bold colours of the artworks. They were the same colours as the earth.

'It's going to be a wonderful show, Mum,' said Lulu.

Chapter 6

Waterfall Reef

The next day, the Bell family was up at sunrise. Mum packed a big bag with snorkels, masks, flippers and towels. Dad packed an esky with fruit, sandwiches and drinks. Mum made sure all the kids had long-sleeved shirts and hats to protect them from the sun. They piled in the car and drove to the house.

Anthony was painting on the verandah. He had added two black whales on the sea. They were marked with grey stripes and spots. Lulu thought they looked majestic.

'Ready to go?' Anthony asked.

They followed Anthony's car to a cove near Ardyaloon. There were several boats dragged up above the high tide mark. The kids all swam while the adults launched the boats. Then everyone piled on board.

Anthony had five nephews on his boat. The Bell family was in the other. Lulu, Rosie and Gus wore life vests and hats. The boats surged off into the turquoise water. The sea foamed and churned behind them.

It was low tide so the reef was exposed. Thousands of sharp black rocks

stuck up from the sea like teeth. The
boats navigated carefully through the
sandbanks and rocks. Anthony pointed
to a little head that had popped up from
the sea. Wise old eyes blinked slowly.

'What is it?' asked Lulu.

'It's a green sea turtle,' called Anthony.

Now Lulu could see its splotchy
green-and-brown shell. Lulu was
delighted. She had never seen a sea turtle
in the wild before.

'Oh!' cried Lulu. 'It's so big.'

The turtle bobbed up and down in the water. It paddled its flippers. It watched Lulu curiously then dived and swam away.

Finally they reached their destination: Waterfall Reef. The top of the reef was as flat as a tabletop. At high tide the reef was under the sea. But when the tide dropped, the water flowed off the top of the reef and onto the lower reef surrounding it. This created a waterfall hundreds of metres wide that tumbled into the sea.

Dad and Anthony anchored the boats. The kids scrambled out. The boys carried their spears. On the lower reef, there were many shallow pools full of fish and stingrays.

Anthony showed the boys how to

take aim and throw. Zac threw his spear
at a large fish. It zipped away in a flash of
silver. The spear floated off harmlessly.

Anthony smiled. 'Good try, Zac.
Let's keep practising.'

The boys practised aiming and
throwing their spears.

Dad preferred to fish his own way.
He cast his fishing line and hook off the
end of the boat. 'I lost the bait again,' he
cried in despair. 'There's a big fish out
there that has stolen my bait three times.'

'A big fish, or perhaps a big shark,' joked Anthony. Dad peered over the side of the boat warily.

The five boys from Goorlil set off in bare feet. They ran and chased across the top reef. They hurled their spears at fish and stingrays. Lulu, Rosie and Gus climbed up after them. The Bell children wore runners to protect their feet from

the sharp rocks. Mum followed more
slowly, carrying her camera.

The kids all stood on the edge of the
reef. They peered over. The water poured
between their feet.

Below them was a lower ledge. This ledge was a few metres wide then dropped away into the deep sea.

Zac scrambled over the edge of the waterfall. His cousins followed, carrying their spears.

'Come down,' invited Zac. 'You can have a shower under the waterfall.'

Lulu clambered down more slowly, using footholds in the rock. Lulu helped Rosie and Gus down too.

The boys dunked under the sheets of sea water pouring off the reef above. They splashed and laughed. The Bell kids joined in.

'It's amazing to think that this will be under the sea soon,' said Lulu.

'Yes, we have to be careful,' said Jacob. 'The tide will turn. Then it comes rushing in. The water rises very quickly.'

Zac stood on the edge of the lower reef. He peered into the deeper sea water. A golden shape flickered past. Suddenly Zac threw himself off the edge.

Lulu got a shock. 'Zac?' she cried.

Zac emerged from the sea laughing. Salt water dripped from his hair and skin.

Pierced on the end of his spear was a large golden fish. The boys all cheered.

'It's a golden trevally,' said Jacob.

'Fish for dinner tonight,' said Zac.

Mum took a photo of Zac proudly holding up his catch. He grinned from ear to ear.

'That was amazing,' said Mum.

Anthony came over. He carried two big fish. 'Well done, Zac. What a great catch. But now we need to get going. The tide has turned and it's coming in fast.'

Chapter 7

Turtle Rescue

Everyone headed back to the boats. Dad carefully packed up his fishing gear and stowed it under the seat. He hadn't caught any fish. Anthony stowed his fish in a bucket.

Dad fired up the engine. To get back to Ardyaloon, they had to navigate in a loop around the rocks and sandbanks. The boats chugged slowly. They were having trouble making headway against the strong rush of the tide.

The water gushed and surged, swirling in eddies. The boat was tossed from side to side. It was a long ride back towards shore.

After a while, Anthony turned his boat towards a small deserted island. It rose straight from the sea, rocky and barren. Lulu could see a small beach of powdery white sand. The rocks were banded in rusty red, topped with a haze of greenery.

Dad followed Anthony's lead. They steered the boats under a rock overhang.

'Look up,' called the boys from the boat in front.

Lulu craned her head upwards. There were paintings on the rocky roof. Figures were marked in red and cream ochre and black charcoal. She could tell they were sea creatures –

54

stingrays, sharks, dolphins, fish, turtles and whales. The whales reminded Lulu of the ones Anthony had painted. Carved deep in the rock were the outlines of boomerangs and spears.

'It's beautiful,' said Mum. 'It feels very ancient in here.'

'Our people have been coming here to fish and hunt for thousands of years,' said Anthony. 'Although in the old days they came on rafts, not with outboard motors!'

'Could I take some photographs of the art?' asked Mum. 'I think it would be interesting to include some photos with the show.'

'Yes,' replied Anthony. He grinned. 'Just as long as you remember to send me some copies of your photos.'

Next stop was the beach for a swim. The beach was littered with dozens of beautiful shells. There were large white clam shells, pale beige bailer shells and delicate purple conch shells.

Dad started digging a hole in the sand with Gus. The other boys took their spears. They scrambled over the rock pools hunting for stingrays.

Lulu pulled out her snorkel, diving mask and flippers from the bag of swimming gear.

'Keep your shirt on, honey bun,' said Mum. 'This sun is strong.'

Lulu splashed into the water. It was clear and clean and calm. Little waves rippled on the shore. She swam out towards the deeper water. Rosie stayed in the shallows with Mum.

'Don't go too far out,' called Mum.

Lulu floated face down. She breathed through the snorkel. She could hear it rumble and bubble. With her diving mask on she could see for metres through the sunlit water. She kicked with her flippers and shot away.

Suddenly Lulu saw a dark shadow. It swam towards her. Lulu breathed in quickly. Her heart thumped. *What was it? Could it be a shark?*

Lulu turned and kicked. In her panic she sucked in sea water through the snorkel.

She coughed and spluttered. Her
arms flailed. Lulu spat out her snorkel.
She stared under the water. *Where was
the shadow?*

It was closer now, and stood out
against the light sand. Lulu recognised
the shape. It wasn't a shark. It was too
round. It was a big sea turtle.

Lulu sighed with relief. But
something was not right. The turtle was
wreathed with a necklace. A necklace
of knotted fishing line.

It was tangled around the turtle's neck and front flipper. As the turtle struggled, the snarled noose pulled tighter. The turtle was slowly being choked.

Lulu took a deep breath. There was no time to waste. She kicked her flippers and dived. Deeper and deeper. Lulu reached the turtle. She wrapped her arms around it. The injured creature didn't struggle.

She turned her face towards the surface. She kicked and swam. The turtle was heavy. She kicked harder. Her breath ached in her chest. Blood pounded in her head. She had to breathe. But the heavy weight was holding her down. She kicked even harder. Lulu was determined not to let go of the turtle.

At last she broke free into the fresh air. Sea water showered from her hair and face.

Lulu blinked in the sudden hot sun. She lifted the turtle's head out of the water so it could breathe. The turtle spat out a spurt of sea water. Lulu sucked in a deep breath herself. It felt good.

'Dad, Dad!' called Lulu. 'There's a turtle that needs help.'

Lulu swam towards the shore. She pushed the turtle along in front of her.

Dad splashed into the water. Together they hauled the injured turtle up on the sand. The turtle lay still.

Dad had his fishing knife attached to his belt. He unsheathed it. Slowly and gently he cut the fishing line away. The line was tough and strong. Lulu held the turtle still on the sand. Zac helped her.

Anthony crouched down beside Zac. He used his own knife to cut from the other side. At last the fishing line fell away.

61

By now everyone had gathered around. The fishing line lay in a tangled heap. There were metres of it. Dad examined the turtle.

'Good work, sweetheart,' Dad said. He grinned at Lulu. 'He's quite weak. It looks like you found him just in time. He is one very lucky turtle.'

Lulu gave a big grin back. She had saved the sea turtle.

'Actually he's a she,' said Anthony. 'You can tell by her front flippers. The male flippers have claws.' He pointed to the turtle's leathery front flipper.

'You won't eat her?' asked Rosie. She looked worried. Lulu's heart gave a lurch.

Anthony laughed. 'No, Rosie. We have plenty of fish for dinner.'

Dad picked up the tangled fishing line. He packed it away in the bag.

'People are so thoughtless,' he said. 'Someone probably threw this overboard without thinking about how dangerous it could be.'

Anthony nodded. 'That can be a big problem. It was probably from a tourist boat.'

He picked up a handful of sand. He rubbed it around the turtle's mottled shell in big circles.

'This is how we clean the turtle's shell. The sand removes the algae and growths. This keeps the turtle healthy. Our kids have to learn how to care for the animals as our people have always done.'

'Turtle dirty,' said Gus. He wrinkled his nose.

All the kids took turns to polish the turtle's shell. Lulu loved the feeling of rubbing sand over the hard shell. They splashed handfuls of water to wash away the sand. The shell sparkled in the sunlight. The turtle stared at Lulu with beady black eyes.

'Now I think she is ready to go back,' said Anthony.

Dad and Anthony picked up the turtle. They carried her out into the water. Lulu followed. The turtle paused,

floating for a moment. Lulu and the
other kids swam beside it. Then the turtle
dived and swam away.

Goodbye, turtle, said Lulu to herself.
Swim hard and stay safe.

Chapter 8

Full Moon

 The next few days whirled past in a blur. The Bell family went swimming, snorkelling, boating and fishing. Pearl took all the girls out gathering oysters and shellfish. She warned them to stay close. The old man saltwater crocodile had been seen swimming nearby.

Mum spent the mornings visiting the artists, talking about their artwork and choosing the very best pieces for the show. She was so happy with the collection.

Finally it was the last day of their stay. The next morning they would get up very early for the drive to the airport. Lulu felt sad. The week had passed so fast.

Pearl and Harry invited everyone to a huge farewell feast to say goodbye. Anthony took the boys out fishing. Pearl took the girls out to collect oysters. Harry took Dad to catch mud crabs.

As the sun went down, the two families gathered around the fire. Everyone had made something to share. There were chunks of fish barbecued over the fire. Hot, smoky damper was cooked in the coals. Pearl had made a big pot of chilli mud crab. Mum had made salads and fried rice. The children had picked mangoes from the old tree.

Everyone sat on camp chairs around
the fire chatting and laughing. They ate
with their fingers from paper plates.
Chilli the pup lay on Lulu's feet.
His tummy was round and fat from
eating scraps.

'This is the best
fish I've ever eaten,'
said Dad.

Lulu licked the crumbs from her fingers. 'Mmm. Food cooked over the fire always tastes best,' she said.

A full moon rose over the sea. Its silvery reflection shimmered on the water. The fire flared up as Harry threw his paper plate on the flames.

Zac stood. He beckoned to the other boys.

'The boys have prepared a special surprise for you,' said Harry. The five boys slipped away into the shadows.

They soon returned wearing bright blue cloths around their waists. Their bodies were painted with bands of white ochre.

They each carried two bark shields. The shields were painted in bright patterns of white, clay-red, blue and black.

Lulu felt a shiver of anticipation.

'The boys are going to dance for you,' explained Harry. 'They are going to dance the story of a great turtle hunt near Sunday Island.'

Harry pointed out in the darkness towards the distant islands. 'A big storm comes in over the sea during the hunt.'

Harry picked up a pair of wooden clapping sticks. He began to beat out the time. Several members of the family started to sing and clap. Lulu couldn't understand the words, but she thought they sounded magical.

The boys danced. They stamped their feet and paddled with their shields. The dance was energetic and beautiful.

Suddenly Lulu smiled. She realised there were now six boys dancing. Five of them wore blue cloths and white ochre marks. One wore red board shorts and white ochre markings. It was Gus. He danced behind Zac, copying his movements.

'Gus, honey bun,' called Mum. 'Come and sit down.'

Harry smiled. 'It's okay,' he said. 'The boys invited him to join in.'

The dancers finished. Everyone burst into applause. Gus bowed.

'Thank you, Harry,' said Mum. 'Thank you, boys. That was wonderful. But now my little chickens need to go to bed. We have a *very* early start in the morning.'

Rosie yawned. Lulu stood up slowly. She didn't want to go to bed yet. She didn't want the last day at Goorlil to end.

Anthony smiled at Lulu. He turned to Mum and Dad.

'Perhaps a little while longer?' said Anthony. 'I think we should walk down to the beach. It's a full moon. That would be a good way to say goodbye to Goorlil.'

Lulu jumped up with excitement. Mum hesitated.

'Great idea,' said Dad. 'The kids can sleep on the plane tomorrow.'

'We'll need to be very quiet,' said Anthony. 'Just in case.'

Just in case what? wondered Lulu.

Everyone followed Anthony down to the beach. He held up his hand to tell them to stop. The sand glowed white by the light of the moon. The sea rippled with a silvery shimmer. Lulu could hear the gentle *lap, lap, lap* of water on the sand.

Anthony crouched down in the sand dune. Everyone followed, crouching in the shadows. Anthony scanned the beach.

'Look,' he whispered. He pointed to the ripple of waves.

Lulu saw a low, dark shape creeping out of the sea. In a moment she realised it was a sea turtle.

The turtle crawled slowly up the beach. Finally she reached the sand dune just a few metres away.

The turtle stopped. She used her four flippers to dig a wide, shallow hole. Then she used her back flippers to dig deeper. It took a long time. The turtle grunted and huffed.

'She's laying her eggs,' whispered Anthony.

Next the turtle used her flippers to cover the eggs. She scattered fine, dry sand over the top to hide the nest.

At last the turtle was finished. She turned and crawled. Slowly, carefully, she inched her way back to the moonlit sea.

Goodbye, sea turtle, thought Lulu. She looked up at the stars. *My wish came true.*

Chapter 9

The Art Show

A few weeks later, it was time for the opening night of the art show. Dad, Lulu, Rosie and Gus arrived at the Shelly Beach Art Gallery. A big sign said 'Welcome to the Goorlil Dreaming Art Show'.

Mum was inside greeting the guests. She wore a gorgeous black lace dress. Lulu and Rosie were wearing their best dresses too.

Mum kissed each of them. Her eyes sparkled. 'Look,' she whispered. 'There are so many people here.'

Lulu stared around. The gallery was crowded. People laughed and chatted and admired the artwork.

The walls were hung with the paintings from Ardyaloon. There were other artworks too: painted shields, clapping sticks, woven baskets, boomerangs and carved spears. The walls glowed with the vibrant colours of the earth.

Beside each of the exhibits were Mum's photos. There were portraits of the artists working. There were photos

of the Ardyaloon landscape. The turquoise sea. The rust-red islands. The scrubby green bush.

There were photos of the Goorlil kids swimming with sharks, spearing fish and gathering oysters. Lulu smiled as she saw pictures of all her Goorlil friends.

'The show looks beautiful, Mum,' said Lulu.

Mum kissed Lulu on the forehead.

'Thanks, honey bun,' she said. 'And
I have a special surprise for you.'

Lulu wondered what Mum's surprise
could be. But there was no time to guess.
Mum stepped up to the microphone. The
crowd fell silent.

'Welcome to Goorlil Dreaming.
Thanks for coming along to this special
showcase,' she said. 'I would like to
welcome a very honoured guest to tell us
about the art and the stories behind it.'

Everyone clapped loudly. A tall
man in a red shirt stepped up to the
microphone. It was Anthony. He winked
at Lulu, Rosie and Gus. So that was
Mum's surprise!

'The history of our art goes back
more than sixty thousand years,' said
Anthony. 'That is five times older than
the Egyptian pyramids.'

Lulu looked at him in surprise. That was *very* old.

'Our art is inspired by the beliefs and magic of the Dreamtime. During the Dreamtime, our ancestral spirits created the animals, plants, people, land and sea.'

Anthony waved at the wall behind him. On it was a canvas covered by a cloth. Together Anthony and Mum pulled the cloth down.

They revealed a huge painting. Two black whales danced together. They were marked with stripes and white dots.

Underneath, nine green sea turtles swam and dived. On the sand were three big turtle nests. The nests were filled with dozens of turtle eggs.

It was Anthony's painting of *Goorlil Dreaming*. Anthony told the gallery the story of the whales and the turtles wooing. Lulu loved hearing the story again.

Then Mum pointed to the photo beside the painting. It showed Anthony, Dad, Zac and Lulu. They were working to free the injured sea turtle from its necklace of tangled fishing line.

'*Goorlil Dreaming* is the ancient story of the sea turtles,' explained Mum. 'This photograph is a new story of sea turtles. It is a story of different people, different families, different generations working together to look after the land and its creatures. It is a story of our future.'

Anthony grinned at Lulu. He gave her a thumbs-up sign.

Lulu grinned back.

It was a story about sea turtles she would never forget.

Author's Note

Lulu Bell and the Sea Turtle was written with the help and support of the Davey and Hunter families of Gambanan.

✴

My family and I were lucky enough to visit the Dampier Peninsula, where we stayed with an Aboriginal family at their outstation near Ardyaloon. The adventures of the Bell family are based on the adventures we had together as a family – making spears, hunting stingray, fishing, hearing traditional stories and looking after sea turtles.

The painting *Goorlil Dreaming* is based on a painting that I have hanging in my office, which was painted for us by an Indigenous artist called Ashley Hunter.

The Bardi people we stayed with were the Daveys and the Hunters — a wonderful family of teachers, artists, hunters and storytellers.

The time we spent with them was one of the most amazing experiences of my life. I would like to thank them for their generosity and hospitality as they shared their culture, stories and way of life with us, and welcomed us into their home and family. We will never forget them.

— Belinda Murrell

Some Bardi Words

aarli – fish

baawa – child

bayalbarr – dolphin

booroo – home

doorba – luck

gadiya – white person

goorlil – turtle

goowa – mermaid

goowid – moon

linygoorr – crocodile

miinimbi – whale

Lulu Bell and the Circus Pup

A circus is setting up near Lulu's house. How exciting! But as Lulu and her family walk past, they see a young girl crying. Stella tells them that Spangles the performing dog is missing.

Lulu is determined to help Stella find the clever pup. Can Stella teach Lulu a circus trick in return? When the show starts, the Bell family might get a big surprise!

Read all the Lulu Bell books

About the Author

Belinda Murrell grew up in a vet hospital and Lulu Bell is based on some of the adventures she shared with her own animals. After studying Literature at Macquarie University, Belinda worked as a travel journalist, editor and technical writer. A few years ago, she began to write stories for her own three children – Nick, Emily and Lachlan. Belinda's books include the Sun Sword fantasy trilogy, timeslip tales *The Locket of Dreams*, *The Ruby Talisman* and *The Ivory Rose*, and Australian historical tales *The Forgotten Pearl* and *The River Charm*.

www.belindamurrell.com.au

About the Illustrator

Serena Geddes spent six years working with a fabulously mad group of talented artists at Walt Disney Studios in Sydney before embarking on the path of picture book illustration in 2009. She works both traditionally and digitally and has illustrated many books, ranging from picture books to board books to junior novels.

www.serenageddes.com.au